FOR SABINE

(With the usual hugs for Monika and Luka)

www.davidmelling.co.uk

www.huglessdouglas.co.uk

HODDER CHILDREN'S BOOKS

First published in Great Britain in 2019
by Hodder and Stoughton

Text and illustrations copyright © David Melling, 2019

The moral rights of the author have been asserted.

A CIP catalogue record for this book
is available from the British Library.

HB ISBN: 978 1 444 93117 4
PB ISBN: 978 1 444 93118 1

1 3 5 7 9 10 8 6 4 2

Printed and bound in China

MIX
Paper from
responsible sources
FSC® C104740

Hodder Children's Books
An imprint of Hachette Children's Group
Part of Hodder and Stoughton
Carmelite House
50 Victoria Embankment
London, EC4Y 0DZ

An Hachette UK Company

www.hachette.co.uk
www.hachettechildrens.co.uk

HUGLESS DOUGLAS

PLAYS HIDE-and-SEEK

David Melling

Hodder Children's Books

Douglas and the sheep
were playing HIDE-AND-SEEK.

Douglas had never played this game before. He loved
hiding, scrunching down into a tight ball, while at the
same time peeping out to see if anyone was coming.

It was so much fun, until Douglas
noticed something …

In every game so far, Douglas was always the first one to be found.

'FOUND YOU!'

'FOUND YOU!'

'FOUND YOU!'

Always!

Eventually, he gave up.
'I don't like hiding anymore.
I can't find anywhere big
enough for all of me!'

'Be a seeker with me.'
said Little Sheep.
'We'll make a great team.'

'You'll have to start again from Counting Rock –
it's only fair!' called Flossie as everyone ran away to hide.

Douglas and Little Sheep counted.

1 2 3 4 5 6 7 8 9 . . .

10!

'Here we come, **READY OR NOT!**'

'I bet I'm a really good seeker!' said Douglas.

Douglas was a good seeker. He found 1,2,3,4,5 sheep all by himself!

He also found Owl, Hedgehog and two ducks – which was a problem because they weren't playing hide-and-seek.

Little Sheep thought
Douglas should put Owl,
Hedgehog and the
ducks back … exactly
where he found them.

'Don't worry, Douglas,'
baa-ed the sheep,
'you found us, fair and square!
Let's go and look for the others.'

'FOUND YOU!
6

'FOUND YOU!
7

'FOUND YOU!
8

'FOUND YOU!
9

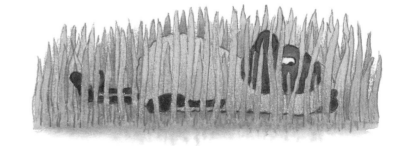

Eventually, they only had Flossie to find.
'But where can she be? We've looked everywhere,'
sighed the sheep.

Everywhere except ...
'Baa Baa Bush!'
cried Douglas.

Douglas was so excited he ran all the way. He picked up Baa Baa Bush and gave it a good shake.

'Yoo-hoo, Flossie, are you in here?'

There was a little
squeak, then ...

out
she
popped!

'FOUND
YOU!'

'1, 2, 3, 4, 5, 6, 7, 8, 9, 10!
That's it, we found **10** sheep.
You're right, Little Sheep, we
do make a great team,'
laughed Douglas.

'Little Sheep?'

Douglas looked around.
Little Sheep had disappeared!
'Little Sheep, where are you?' he called.

They were all worried. It was getting late and
they needed to find their friend before it got dark.

They searched everywhere. Finally they spotted a trail
of leaves and decided to follow it. It led all the way back to …

... Counting Rock.

And there, sitting on top,
was Little Sheep.

Everyone cheered.
'We thought we'd lost you,' said Douglas.

'You did!' Little Sheep smiled bravely.
'The Baa Baa Bush landed on me and when
I wriggled out I was on my own, but I knew
you'd find me if I came back here.'

'You clever Little Sheep!'
smiled Douglas.

They all gathered around in
a circle and gave each other a

LOST-AND-
FOUND
HUG!

TOP TIPS FOR HIDE-AND-SEEK

Try not to get stuck in
your hiding place

Closing your eyes is
NOT hiding

Closing the seeker's eyes
is also NOT hiding

Camouflage yourself

Use a cunning disguise (works best in a crowd)

Hide behind something big
(and try not to laugh)

Ask your friends to help you hide

Count quickly

Find somewhere high up to see over a larger area

Look for clues

Beware of tricks

Don't get cross if you can't find anyone

Look in tricky underground places

HOTTER, COLDER!

Hotter, Colder is another fun hiding game!
You will need two or more people to play.

The rules are simple:

1. One person leaves the room while the other players **HIDE** an object; a cake, for example.

2. When the object is hidden, the **FINDER** comes back into the room and begins searching.

3. The other players help guide the finder by calling **HOTTER** when they move closer to where the object is hidden, or **COLDER** when they move farther away.

4. Once the object is **FOUND**, a **NEW PLAYER** has a turn.

WARM   HOT   HOTTER!

FREEZING!   COLDER   COLD